ASH CLIMBS THE RANKS

ADAPTED BY JEANETTE LANE

SCHOLASTIC INC.

ISBN 978-1-338-67085-1

10 9 8 7 6 5 4 3 2 1   23 24 25 26 27

Printed in the U.S.A.   40

First printing 2023

CHAPTER ONE

For as long as Ash Ketchum could remember, he'd had the same goal. Every single day, he had been on the same ultimate mission: to become a Pokémon Master. Sunup to sundown. Some of his friends had even accused him of thinking about Pokémon battles twenty-four hours a day! (Ash insisted that was impossible—he needed at least ten hours of sleep every day, so he could only really train for fourteen hours.)

But when Professor Cerise offered Ash and Goh tickets to the World Coronation Series Finals, things changed for Ash.

Before that point, Ash hadn't even known that such a long, involved tournament existed—a tournament with Trainers from all over, with Pokémon of every

type. The whole crew at Professor Cerise's lab had been excited to get to explain it to him.

Ren, one of Professor Cerise's lab assistants, looked at Ash over his red-rimmed glasses. "Up until now, each region has had its own League, or Championship, each with its own Champion," Ren had told him. He pulled up the info on his computer. The screen showed an amazing world-class arena, bigger than any stadium Ash had ever seen.

"But at the World Coronation Series, they choose the best from everyone around the world," Chrysa added. She smiled at Ash, knowing he would be totally into the whole idea of the World Coronation Series.

"That *is* cool," Ash agreed. It was the best of the best!

"And these are for the finals!" Goh emphasized, holding the ticket right in front of his face, as if he didn't believe it was real. "Tickets for the big showdown!" Of course, Goh already knew about the World Coronation Series. Goh made it a point of knowing every fact and detail about all things Pokémon. Even when he was six and in his first-ever Pokémon camp with Professor Oak, Goh had known enough to practically lead the camp!

"That means we'll get to see the world's best Pokémon battle for ourselves!" Ash exclaimed. His mind was blown!

Professor Cerise, who always wore a white lab coat with the collar turned up, had spent his career learning about Pokémon. He was the professor at a

laboratory in Vermilion City. The lab was new, with top-of-the-line equipment. There, the team gathered as much information as possible to uncover the mysteries of Pokémon.

Professor Cerise had taken on both Ash and Goh as research fellows. It was an amazing opportunity for the two friends because they were able to travel all over to discover more about their favorite subject—Pokémon! While they were in Vermilion City, they were staying with Professor Cerise.

Both Ash and Goh were helping the professor. The tournament tickets were a special way for him to thank them. "There are things that will happen in that stadium that will awe and amaze you!" Professor Cerise told the two Pokémon fans. The professor knew that the tournament finals would take place in the Galar region. And, being a top researcher, Professor Cerise knew that the Trainers in Galar had some unique skills when it came to big-time battling.

And the battle didn't disappoint! The Galar region happened to be the home of Leon, one of the final two competitors. Leon had won the Galar Champion Cup on his very first try in battles that weren't even close. The tournament announcer had all kinds of fancy names for Leon, like the Superstar of Galar and King of the Kingdom. Ash and Goh thought Leon probably deserved those names—he was undefeated, after all.

Leon's opponent, Lance, had an impressive winning record as well. He was one of the Kanto region's Elite Four, winner of the prestigious Elite Four Cup, and the victor at the Pokémon World Tournament in Driftveil City.

Before the battle, the two competitors met in the center for their introductions. Wyndon Stadium was the biggest that Ash had ever seen, yet the personalities of the two competing Trainers easily filled the arena.

"I've seen your previous battles," Lance said to Leon. He wore a long black cape and had a serious expression, his eyes narrowed. "I can tell you're a Trainer with considerable skill. That's why I imagined that you would be the one to eventually join me here."

"Can you feel it, Lance?" Leon asked with a dramatic flair. "To witness the tense, still air on the pitch?" He told his opponent that the audience was there to see one of them win, and one of them lose. "I love pushing past the fear. I love giving it everything I've got as a Trainer. It's the greatest feeling, and I can't get enough of it."

Up in the stands, Ash couldn't get enough of it either. He knew exactly what Leon was talking about. It was exactly how Ash felt about battling!

"The reason I'm unbeatable," Leon went on, "is because I learn from every battle I see or take part in, and today, I'll learn from my victory."

Leon and Lance were very well matched. It was already an incredible contest between Lance's Gyarados and Leon's Charizard. Between Hyper Beams and Flamethrowers and Air Slashes and Dragon Dance, Ash couldn't imagine a better battle. Then something massive happened. When the Trainers came to a standstill, when their Pokémon had used all their moves, both Trainers boosted the size and power of the Pokémon they had on the battlefield. With elite bands, they were

able to superpower their Pokémon. The oversized versions of their Pokémon, Dynamax Gyarados and Gigantamax Charizard, produced moves as huge as they were! It was literally the biggest battle the friends had ever seen.

Hometown favorite Leon and his undefeated Charizard were the winners. Leon was declared the World Coronation Series Monarch. And, after seeing the pure skill in that battle, Ash declared a new mission: He wanted to battle the world's best. He wanted to battle Leon!

CHAPTER TWO

Pikachu scowled at Ash.

"That's enough, buddy," Ash explained, taking the snack bag from his partner. "You've had plenty already." Then he looked back out the plane window. As usual, he was already anticipating the battles that would take place when they reached the stadium in Shalour City.

"It's my first time in Kalos!" Goh exclaimed. "I say we catch a bunch of Pokémon!"

Raboot mumbled a response but didn't seem all that excited. Raboot seemed to know that Goh saw just about everything as the chance to catch new Pokémon!

Then Goh looked across the airplane aisle to his friend. "You'd better win the Battle Festival Challenge!"

"For sure," Ash agreed. "And I'll *keep* winning!"

"*Pika!*" chimed in his partner.

If there was a day to keep winning, this was it! The Battle Festival Challenge was an event where Trainers could raise their World Coronation Series ranking in one fell swoop. Many Trainers had come to the stadium, and competitors could challenge just about anyone, so it was an important day for Trainers to be at their best.

As for Ash, he had been on a winning streak in the World Coronation Series, and he felt ready to move up in the rankings. In fact, he was closing in on the next level. If the day went as he hoped, he could leave the entry level, the Normal Class, behind for good.

By now, Ash had a good rhythm going. It felt like another life, back when he didn't know anything about the World Coronation Series. Even after he and Goh had gone to watch Lance and Leon in the finals, Goh had to sit Ash down and explain it all.

Ash knew that he wanted to battle Leon and that he'd have to enter the World Coronation Series to do it. But Goh knew Ash didn't realize just how many battles it would take for him to be able to log an official battle with Leon. And when Ash found out there were over ten thousand Trainers competing in the series? Everyone at Professor Cerise's lab had to give Ash a pep talk. At some point, Goh had

shown Ash a diagram, just so he would understand the different classes. Everyone starts in Normal, then those who win a certain number of battles move on to Great, then Ultra. Only the final elite eight are in the Master Class. These days, Ash always knew his ranking. He was becoming a pro at this!

At the suggestion of everyone in the lab, Ash had found his first battle right in Vermilion City. "A Trainer's momentum depends on how well they do in their first match," Professor Cerise had said. "That first battle's important."

The more Ash heard, the more game he was. And

his Pokémon were, too! "All I have to do is win, win, win!" he said.

Ren advised that to boost his rankings in one shot, Ash should battle someone whose ranking was already high. No matter what success a Trainer or Gym Leader has had, they all enter the World Coronation Series at the same level.

The local acting Gym Leader was also competing in the World Coronation Series, and Ash set his sights on battling him first: Visquez. It had turned out to be an intense two-on-two battle between Visquez's Raichu and Electrode and Ash's Pikachu and Gengar. Even though it was a Normal-Class battle, there was

nothing normal about the Trainers' skills or battle plans! Visquez, who wore a military-green cropped vest and combat boots, had trained her Pokémon to have razor-sharp technique. But, as always, Ash had some clever tricks up his short sleeves. His unexpected moves led him to a win, which took his rank to 3,763.

"You kept surprising me with strategies I could *never* dream up!" Goh had said afterward. "You had me on the edge of my seat!"

From then on, Ash looked for and accepted battles whenever he could. He even went up against his friend Oliver during a special orienteering session for Professor Cerise. The kids he was teaching that day loved watching the battle—and Ash loved being able to show them how much a battle can help Trainers learn about and bond with their Pokémon. He also loved seeing his rank go up to 1,512!

The Battle Festival Challenge was another great opportunity. There were so many battles back-to-back, with Pokémon of all shapes and sizes. Ash was ready to go! The stadium had four separate battling arenas, so there was always

plenty of action. And the crowd! The fans clapped
and cheered for their favorites. Even early in
the day, the seats were all full. It was an electric
atmosphere—perfect to charge up an Electric-type
Pokémon for victory!

*"Welcome to the grass battlefield, where
Pikachu and Clawitzer are in a heated battle!"* the
festival announcer said over the loudspeaker.
The announcer told the fans that it would be a one-on-
one battle, where each Trainer could use only one
Pokémon.

Ash and Pikachu stared across the battle pitch
at their next opponent. The sea-blue, Water-type

Pokémon had two sharp pincer claws. One was much larger than the other. Clawitzer's partner was a tall man named Rob who wore a western hat, blue jeans, and a vest.

"All right, Clawitzer, Flash Cannon!" Rob yelled with a distinct drawl.

"Pikachu, use Thunderbolt!" Ash directed. Pikachu somersaulted in the air and drew up the energy for a powerful Thunderbolt. Pikachu aimed it right at Clawitzer. It was an exact hit, but Clawitzer just opened its larger claw wide and took in all that electric energy.

"Look at that! Clawitzer just swallowed that

Thunderbolt attack with its claw!" the festival
announcer pointed out. "That Electric-type attack
should've caused real damage. What happened?"

Ash wondered the same thing.

"Flash Cannon absorbed the energy from your
Electric-type move," Rob bragged. "How do you like
that?"

On the other end of the pitch, Ash was perplexed,
but he knew he couldn't let it slow him down. "If
that move didn't work, use Iron Tail!" Ash called to
Pikachu.

"Use Crabhammer!" Rob demanded to Clawitzer.

Pikachu immediately leaped forward and bounded
into the air. As Clawitzer was still charging up its

claw, Pikachu crashed down onto the Water-type Pokémon. Pikachu's zigzag Iron Tail gleamed bright with power as it made contact, knocking out its opponent!

"Clawitzer . . ." Rob cried out.

Almost instantly, a neon green Drone Rotom buzzed down from the sky. It hovered over the two Pokémon before declaring, "Clawitzer is unable to battle, so the victory goes to Ash of Pallet Town!"

"Yeah, we did it, Pikachu!" Ash cheered.

Rob scowled as he reached out to return his Pokémon to its Poké Ball. "'Kay, Ash. I won't forget that name," he muttered, shaking his head.

"That's Ash's third straight win!" the announcer told the crowd. *"A fourth win will put him into Great Class! Pretty exciting!"*

CHAPTER THREE

Meanwhile, Goh had traveled from the rocky seaside to lush meadows to a forest dense with underbrush. He knew which Pokémon he was most likely to track down in each area. All along, Raboot was loyally at his side. At times the Fire-type Pokémon was even impressed with its partner's skill and good fortune.

"Poké Ball, go!" Goh yelled again and again. "Go! Go! Go!" From the Two-Handed Pokémon, Binacle, to a blue Flabébé to tiny Fletchling with its distinctive markings, Goh had kept his Rotom Phone busy identifying all his new acquisitions. Goh didn't tire of throwing Poké Balls, but he finally decided to make his way toward the stadium.

"It's time we head on over to cheer for Ash," he said

to Raboot—but in the next breath, yelled, "Look! It's a Red Flower Flabébé!" It couldn't hurt to capture more Pokémon on his way to the tournament, could it?

Outside the stadium, Ash was giving a pep talk to all of the Pokémon that were traveling with him. Dragonite, Gengar, and Riolu crowded around their Trainer, and Pikachu was in its regular perch on Ash's shoulder.

"With one more win, we'll reach the Great Class," Ash said. "Thanks to you guys!" The whole crew seemed excited by their success and also grateful

that Ash recognized their training and strong efforts.
"Let's give it all we've got!" Ash encouraged them.

Suddenly, Riolu grunted and pricked its ears, staring into the distance. It sensed something the others could not see. Then it ran off.

"Riolu!" Ash cried.

When the others finally caught up, Riolu had stopped. It seemed to be waiting for something. In an instant, another Pokémon appeared. A Lucario. Its eyes were closed, but it was sending out pulses of energy.

Pikachu stood up on its hind legs and waved its paws. *"Pika, Pikachu!"*

The Lucario let out a friendly chuckle.

"Lucario?" Ash whispered, still trying to figure out

exactly what was happening. "Hey, I think I know that Lucario . . ."

"Yoo-hoo!" came a call from behind them. Ash turned around to see someone Rollerblading in his direction, a long blonde ponytail streaming behind her.

"Hi, Ash!"

"Korrina! I knew it! I could feel it—Lucario's Aura," Ash explained.

"Pika, pika!" his Pokémon added.

"It's been forever!" Korrina said in her usual bubbly way. "Good to see you, Pikachu!" she greeted Pikachu with a friendly pat. "How've you been?"

"Pikachu." It was clear the Electric-type Pokémon was excited to see an old friend.

Next, Korrina turned to Ash's other Pokémon and smiled. "My name's Korrina, and I'm the Shalour City Gym Leader. And this is my partner, Lucario!" Without missing a beat, Korrina kneeled down. "So you caught a Riolu?" she asked Ash. It made sense that she was curious, since Riolu evolves into Lucario.

"Yeah, it hatched from an Egg," Ash told Korrina.

"You stick with Ash," Korrina advised the young Fighting type. "He'll make you super strong."

Lucario grunted.

"*Rioluuu!*" Riolu looked up to Lucario with a shy smile.

Korrina stood back up and started talking to the group again. "I met Ash a while back, and the two of us had quite a Gym battle!"

"I just happened to win," Ash added, with a clench of his fist.

"So, that's it, huh?" Korrina said, calling out Ash. He had always been so obsessed with battle success, and Korrina knew it!

"Well, that's what counts!" Ash insisted. "Ooh, are you in the Battle Festival Challenge, too?"

"Of course!" Korrina answered. "But today, I'm not here as a Gym Leader. I'm just another challenger. Winning my way to take on Leon!"

Ash's jaw dropped. Korrina was the first Trainer he'd found who was also aiming to challenge the reigning Monarch, just like Ash!

"This is why Lucario and I have been training as hard as we have been! To win, and win, and win some more, and move up the rankings! And with my very next victory, I'll rank up and enter the Great Class!" She held up her Rotom Phone as proof. She then turned to Ash with a knowing smile. "You too, right?"

Ash grinned. "Let's have a battle, and the winner will get to do just that!" What great stakes for a battle!

"Pika!" Pikachu was excited, too.

"Riolu?" Ash said, getting the young Pokémon's

attention. "Watch Lucario and its style of battling." At once, Riolu took a fighting posture, throwing punches at the air. Ash laughed at Riolu's attitude—it was always pumped up. "I just want you to check it out for now."

Then Ash looked Pikachu in the eye. "Keep an eye on Riolu, 'kay?"

"Pika pika." Pikachu jumped down from Ash's shoulder and stood by Riolu's side.

Ash knew it was an amazing opportunity for Riolu to learn from Korrina's veteran partner, and he trusted Pikachu to keep Riolu on the sidelines.

In a nearby forest, Goh had his own surprise run-in with a Lucario. Goh and Raboot had been chasing after the Red Flower Flabébé and found themselves in a forest clearing. They were both out of breath, and the Flabébé had vanished.

"Anything out there?" Goh asked. Raboot lifted its ears and arms, scanning the area. It shook its head. "Wow, not a trace?" Goh said with a sigh.

But then Raboot shot into the air with a twirl and did Ember, kicking the flaming mass of ember into the bushes. As soon as it hit the underbrush, a Lucario burst out, striking a fighting pose.

"Lucario?" Goh said in surprise, lifting his arm to aim a Poké Ball.

"Your reaction shows promise," said a man who appeared behind the Fighting-type Pokémon. The man was calm and had very, very long eyebrows. A gentle smirk played at the sides of his mouth.

"Hold on," Goh said, realizing something. "You're its Trainer?" Goh was suddenly embarrassed.

The man laughed.

"Sorry, I thought it was a wild Lucario," Goh admitted.

"I'm sorry to disappoint you. But you've got spirit, and I like that," the man said kindly. "Is this your first encounter with one?"

"That's right. We've come here to catch lots of Pokémon. Since it's my first trip to Kalos, I wanted to catch a whole bunch!" Goh could not hide his enthusiasm for his mission. He and Ash had that in common!

"Well, how many have you caught?" the man asked.

The two examined Goh's Rotom Phone to see the day's bounty.

"Remarkable! You've managed to catch so many Flabébé with different-colored flowers!" There were lots of nods of approval. "And catching an orange one is quite an impressive feat."

"I'm still working on white," Goh told him.

"They say that white is extremely hard to find! I don't think one's been seen around here . . ." The man's voice trailed off.

"Are you familiar with this area?" Goh asked, hoping to get some hints.

"You could say so. My granddaughter's battling in the stadium over there today." The man nodded in the direction of the giant arena. "I thought I'd go and see how she's doing."

"No way! My good friend's competing in it right now! He came here from Kanto to battle, while I came to catch Pokémon."

"I haven't met anyone from there in quite a while. Not since I met a friend of my granddaughter's named Ash . . ."

"Ash?!"

"Yes, that's right," the man said thoughtfully. "His partner was Pikachu."

"That's the guy I was talking about!" Goh exclaimed.

What were the chances? It only seemed fitting that the two new friends would go watch the tournament together.

CHAPTER FOUR

"**N**ow, on the rock battlefield, we will have a Normal Class battle," Drone Rotom announced to the crowd. Its mechanical voice was quite loud for its tiny, insect-like body. "And it's Ash versus Korrina! For today's battle, each can use two Pokémon."

Ash and Korrina stood on either side of the rocky field.

"Listen to the crowd roar!" the announcer called. *"They're cheering for their beloved Shalour City Gym Leader, Korrina!"*

Korrina waved up at the stands, smiling.

"She'll be facing off against an up-and-comer from the Kanto region—Ash!" the announcer added.

Ash touched the bill of his baseball hat. "All right, let's do this . . ."

He was ready to face the local favorite. His Riolu and Pikachu were encouraging him from the sidelines— though they both would rather be in on the action!

"Riolu!" Korrina called across the battlefield to Ash's young Fighting type.

Its ears pricked up from the front row of the stands.

"Be sure to cheer for my Lucario, okay?!" Korrina suggested. "You'll see something cool if you do!"

"What are you talking about, Korrina?" Ash demanded, annoyed. "You *know* Riolu's gonna be cheering for us!"

Ash took a deep breath. It felt funny, having both Riolu and Pikachu in the stands for such an important match.

And what was Korrina getting at? What kind of cool stunt were she and Lucario going to pull? Korrina was always energetic and clever, especially in the battle ring. And it was easy to see her connection with Lucario was strong. Just what did she have up her sleeve?

At the arena entrance, as the doors slid open, Goh and his new friend, whose name was Gurkinn, were in for a surprise of their own.

"Look over there!" yelled Goh, pointing. "It's Ash!"

"I must say, I'm amazed," Gurkinn admitted. "He's up against my granddaughter!"

With over ten thousand Trainers competing in the World Coronation Series, they hadn't expected Goh's traveling companion and Gurkinn's granddaughter to be battling each other!

The best they could do was hope for a good match, which it would undoubtedly be. How wonderful to see the meeting of two such formidable opponents, both devoted to their Pokémon and the ideals of being a dedicated Trainer!

As the crowd turned its attention to the rock

battlefield, the Drone Rotom buzzed down to the center of the pitch. "Will both competitors please bring out your Pokémon? Thank you!"

Korrina and Ash readied their Poké Balls.

"Three . . . two . . . one . . ." the Drone Rotom counted down. "Go!"

"Yeah!" Ash and Korrina exclaimed at once.

Ash's Gengar and Korrina's Mienshao appeared and were instantly ready to bring their best.

Up in the stands, Goh was making sure he knew all the details on Ash's competition by checking his Rotom Phone. "Mienshao," Goh's phone said. "The Martial Arts Pokémon. A Fighting type. Mienshao

uses the fur on its arms to attack at speeds too fast for the human eye to see."

"Wow. Mienshao," Ash said with a sigh of admiration, taking in the Pokémon's martial-arts-style poise. "It's the very image of a Fighting type!"

And then the Drone Rotom called out its familiar cry, "Battle begin!"

"Use Acrobatics!" Korrina yelled without hesitation.

Mienshao launched into a tumbling pass and double-slapped Gengar.

Gengar's back slammed against a huge boulder. Gengar took the impact with a grunt, squeezing its eyes shut.

"That's fast," Ash observed, caught off guard.

"And the rock battlefield bout begins!" The festival announcer sounded as excited as the fans. *"But Gengar isn't able to dodge Mienshao's lightning-fast Acrobatics!"*

Gone was the mischievous grin from Gengar's face.

"Gengar, are you all right?" Ash cried from the far end of the battlefield. When his Pokémon got up and shook it off, Ash acted quickly. "Gengar, use Psychic!"

With the power of Psychic, Gengar lifted a large rock into the air.

"Use U-Turn," directed Korrina.

Gengar focused its Psychic power and blasted the hunk of rock at Mienshao.

But the Fighting-type Pokémon launched itself into the air and vaulted off the rock. Then it did a graceful aerial flip and aimed for Gengar, kicking it between the eyes.

"Gengar!" Ash called again, worried.

At once, Mienshao returned to Korrina, disappearing from the battlefield, and Lucario appeared in its place.

"And there's the U-Turn switch!" the announcer chimed in to explain the unusual move. *"Mienshao is instantly replaced with Korrina's second Pokémon, Lucario!"*

This move was news to Goh. He looked at Gurkinn. "So, she can use a move to switch out her Pokémon?!"

"Yes, it was a wise decision," said her proud grand-father.

The move was so smooth. It offered Korrina such flexibility, being able to swap her Pokémon with so little effort. Goh realized they all must be so attuned to one another, so in synch. He was astonished.

Ash, however, didn't have the time to be impressed. Gengar was struggling. "Hang in there, Gengar!" called Ash.

"Use Bone Rush!" Korrina directed, crossing her arms and then lifting them high. Lucario held out its arms, and two bones glowing with blue light appeared. The Aura Pokémon began to spin the bones like copter blades, then rushed at Gengar.

"Dodge it and use Shadow Ball!" Ash said, trying to counter Korrina's breakneck offensive attacks. Gengar jumped out of the way and tossed several Shadow Balls at Lucario.

The Aura Pokémon brushed off the attack and followed up with several Bone Rush moves, all making impact. It was too much for the Shadow Pokémon. Gengar was knocked out! Its red eyes were filled with the telltale black swirl, and it wasn't long before the Drone Rotom declared Gengar unable to battle.

"It appears Gengar was completely outmaneuvered," observed the festival announcer. He was stating the obvious to everyone in attendance. Gengar had not had an answer for either Mienshao's or Lucario's moves. *"That's Gym Leader Korrina for you! Using a combination by switching Mienshao with Lucario!"*

"That was so fast," Goh lamented. "There wasn't even enough time for Ash and Gengar to counterattack."

"That's one of Korrina's real strengths," Gurkinn stated. "She and her Pokémon act as one, without a single crack in their defense."

Goh could tell Korrina was skilled, but he still had faith in Ash.

"Gengar, return!" Ash called, holding out a Poké Ball. "You did an awesome job."

"And with Lucario switched out for now, Mienshao's up once again!" the announcer pointed out. *"Those two haven't received so much as a scratch! With Ash backed into a corner, what Pokémon will he bring out next?!"*

CHAPTER FIVE

"'**K**ay . . . Let's go!" Ash yelled, tossing a Poké Ball into the air with a smile.

"Ash's second Pokémon is Dragonite!" confirmed the announcer.

"Gr-aaah!" Dragonite yelled as it stretched its wings and then landed on a red-clay rock.

"I have no complaints about this opponent," Korrina said to herself with confidence. "Are you ready to go?" she checked with Mienshao.

This time, Ash was quick to make the first move. "All right, Dragon Claw!"

Dragonite's fists filled with a powerful green energy.

Korrina responded by calling for a High Jump Kick, and Mienshao leaped forward. The two Pokémon met

and clashed in midair, the strength of their moves even.

"Use Double Slap!" yelled Korrina.

"Use Dragon Dance!" countered Ash.

Mienshao kept coming at Dragonite as the Dragon Pokémon spun higher and higher.

The festival announcer tried to explain the action on the field, but it was fast and intense. *"None of Mienshao's Double Slaps can stop Dragonite's Dragon Dance! On the contrary, those Double Slaps only seem to speed up the Dragon Dance!"*

"Oh!" Goh couldn't believe it, either. "Dragon Dance is only supposed to be a power-up move! I've never seen it protect from attacks." Dragonite twirled so

fast, it looked like it might corkscrew right out of the stadium. When it landed, it looked fierce with fighting energy.

"That Dragon Dance seems to have upped Dragonite's speed and attack strength!" the announcer observed.

"How about that?" asked Ash.

"How about *this*?" Korrina retorted. "Use High Jump Kick!"

Ash asked Dragonite to challenge that with Dragon Claw.

Mienshao came in headfirst, and then Dragonite made a slash with its sharp claws. Its arms glowed with mystical power.

"Dragonite's counterattack was fast," said the announcer. *"It looks like that Dragon Dance is taking full effect!"*

Once the dust cleared, Drone Rotom zipped down to the field and declared that Mienshao was unable to battle.

"Way to go, Dragonite!" Ash cheered. The dual Dragon- and Flying-type Pokémon stood tall with triumphant pride.

Now both Korrina and Ash had a win.

"That Dragon Dance really turned things around!" the announcer exclaimed.

"Mienshao, return now!" Korrina called. "Lucario, it's up to you!" She threw a Poké Ball toward the battlefield, and Lucario appeared in a ready pose. "You know, Ash? I knew battling you would get me fired up!"

"I feel the same way, too!" Ash replied. "But now it's time to show us what Lucario can do!"

"*This* is where it begins," Korrina's grandfather said to Goh.

"Oh, what do you mean by that?" Goh asked.

"Here we go . . ." Korrina cried.

Lucario grunted in agreement.

"Unlock . . ." Korrina yelled, "the power within . . ."

Korrina began a sequence of martial-arts-style punches and kicks, before yelling, "Mega Evolve!" As she finished the fluid moves, a yellow energy surged from her hands. The energy surrounded Lucario as it struck a battle pose, and then it began to transform

the Pokémon. A vibration came from it, shaking the very floor of the stadium.

The fans in the bleachers held their breath, mesmerized by the pulsing light.

"Mega Evolution," Goh whispered, almost not believing it.

"Your first encounter?" Gurkinn asked.

"Yeah," Goh admitted. "I've certainly read and heard about it, and knew it existed . . ."

"Mega Evolution is a phenomenon discovered in the Kalos region that releases a Pokémon's hidden power," Gurkinn explained. "It occurs when Trainer and Pokémon have developed a deep bond of trust."

Down on the floor of the arena, Ash could sense that Dragonite was as overwhelmed as the rest of the stadium. "Don't worry, Dragonite! We'll just keep on battling!"

Ash had seen the transformation before. He had even battled against Pokémon that were Mega Evolved. While it was a commanding use of force, Ash knew he and Dragonite could still defeat it.

Dragonite responded with a determined growl.

"Great! Use Dragon Dance!" Ash yelled.

Dragonite vaulted into the air and began to spin, fast enough to create a whirlwind around its yellow-scaled body. The move had worked against Mienshao, so it was worth trying again. Sure enough, Dragon Dance boosted Dragonite's speed and attack with every turn.

"I'm surprised! You don't normally battle cautiously," Korrina said, criticizing Ash's plan. "Aura Sphere!"

Mega Lucario held out its paws, and an orb filled with neon blue beams of light appeared. Mega Lucario aimed the sphere.

"Fly out of there, Dragonite!" Ash advised. Dragonite quickly took to the sky, swooping all around.

"Those aerial moves are toying with Mega Lucario!" the announcer said.

"You can't avoid Aura Sphere like that!" Korrina demanded. She knew that Aura Sphere was a blast of aura power from deep within the Pokémon's body, and it was almost certain to hit. Korrina doubled down on the move. "Go!"

"Use Hyper Beam!" Ash called. Dragonite began to power up the move, but Aura Sphere caught up to it too soon. Mega Lucario's move slammed into Dragonite with a blast. A cloud of smoke filled the sky, and Dragonite began to fall backward toward the ground.

"Right on the mark!" the festival announcer said. *"Dragonite didn't fire Hyper Beam in time."*

"Let's give it the big one!" Korrina yelled, seeing an opportunity. "Use Power-Up Punch!" Mega Lucario sped after Dragonite, pounding the Dragon Pokémon as it fell. Dragonite hit the ground with a dusty thud.

"Dragonite!" Ash yelled. Pikachu and Riolu watched from the bleachers, their eyes big with worry.

"Are you okay, Dragonite?!" Ash surveyed the far end of the battlefield. Dragonite was pulling itself up and shaking off its wings. What a relief! The Pokémon was ready for another round! "Mega Evolution's real powerful stuff," Ash admitted to himself. "So, what next?" It didn't take him long to come up with an answer. "Wait a sec. I know how we'll take care of this! Hurricane!"

Dragonite began flapping its wings. The motion churned up a mighty wind.

Mega Lucario did its best to shield itself from the wind—and all the rocks that it carried.

"Now give it as much as you've got!" Ash cheered on Dragonite.

"Mega Lucario's being overcome by those Hurricane-force winds!" came the voice of the announcer.

"Not again," murmured Korrina.

"It's perfect! Just what we wanted!" Ash cried.

"Here we go! Ash's unpredictability!" Goh commented, proud of his friend's clever strategy. Next to Goh, Gurkinn wondered how his granddaughter would react to such an unexpected move.

"We're far from beat," Korrina insisted. "Let's show them what I mean. Aura Sphere!"

Mega Lucario used Aura Sphere to counter Hurricane, and the blast threw Dragonite backward.

"Mega Lucario escaped the wind," said the announcer.

"Use Power Punch!" Korrina yelled.

"Use Dragon Claw!" Ash cried.

Both Pokémon screamed with effort as they came at each other, landing their moves. They both fell, collapsing in clouds of dust. And then they both rose back up to their feet.

"But they both have taken a lot of damage," the announcer observed. *"Can they go on?"*

Suddenly, with a grunt, Lucario's feet fell out from under its body.

"Lucario's down!" said the announcer, and Rotom Drone zipped in to announce that the Fighting-type Pokémon was unable to battle.

"Which means the victory goes to Ash of Pallet Town!"

Despite all the effort of Korrina and Lucario, Ash had come out on top!

Ash could hardly believe it. He whimpered before he whooped for joy!

"Pikachu!" his partner cried, and bounded out into the battle ring and leaped onto his shoulder. Ash hurried over to Dragonite. "All right! You're the best! Thanks!" Ash said to the Dragon Pokémon. Dragonite wrapped its arms around Ash in response . . . with a

little too much enthusiasm! "Take it easy!" Ash begged, but Dragonite's hug knocked Ash clear off his feet. "You're amazing. You know that?" Ash groaned from underneath his Pokémon.

Meanwhile, Riolu was not there to celebrate with the rest of its team. Instead, it had headed to the other side of the rock battlefield.

Korrina was praising her Pokémon. "You were amazing, Lucario," she said. Lucario gave a rough sigh.

Only then did the Trainer and Pokémon realize that they were being watched. Riolu stared at Lucario in awe.

"Sorry, I guess that wasn't as cool as I thought it would be," Korrina said to Riolu.

"Rioluuu!" The Emanation Pokémon did not agree! Riolu had its paws up, barely able to keep its excitement inside. This was the first time it had been able to watch a Lucario, its evolved form, in battle. And, despite what Korrina might have thought, Lucario's skill and power did not disappoint!

The win had moved Ash up in the rankings. He was now ranked 921.

"You've made it to the Great Class," Gurkinn said to him later that day. "Excellent."

"Thank you very much," Ash responded.

They were all gathered outside the stadium.

"There's always next time, Korrina," Gurkinn said to his granddaughter.

"We're just getting warmed up," said Korrina with her signature enthusiasm. "Right, Lucario?" Lucario grunted in agreement.

Goh couldn't hold in his excitement any longer. "You were amazing!" he said to Ash. "It took my breath away!"

"That's because Dragonite kept hanging in there," Ash said, not willing to claim all the credit. "So, how did it go for you?" he asked.

Just as Goh started to pull out his Rotom Phone to show Ash, something flitted by.

"A White Flower Flabébé!" Gurkinn pointed out.

"Yes, Raboot! Let's go!" Goh yelled, already hot on the rare Pokémon's trail.

"Raboot," his Pokémon replied, following him.

It had been a rewarding day for Ash and Goh . . . and their Pokémon!

CHAPTER SIX

As Ash and Goh continued their adventures, they both kept their eyes on their chosen prize. Ash signed up for more World Coronation Series battles, and Goh searched for new Pokémon everywhere they went.

Now with a rank of 890, Ash remained undefeated. He had not lost one tournament battle! As he and Goh headed to Saffron City, the home of the famous Fighting Dojo, Ash felt unbeatable!

The Fighting Dojo offered something for Goh, too. At the dojo, they trained two different Fighting Pokémon, and visitors could select one to add to their collection.

Ash stood with one of the dojo's Trainers, watching Riolu spar in a practice bout. Riolu was exchanging mighty punches with a Hitmonchan. Then

it immediately took on a Hitmonlee with acrobatic aerial kicks. The dojo Trainer observed how well Riolu battled the dojo's elite Fighting-type Pokémon.

"Hmmm. Good movements," the black-belt Trainer said.

"I know, right?" Ash agreed. "It feels like we're on a roll and we're gonna win everything!"

"*Pikachu!*" Ash's partner enthusiastically agreed from its usual spot atop Ash's shoulder.

"Remember, you're in the Fighting Dojo. I wouldn't talk too big," the black-belt Trainer advised. "There isn't a strategy in the world that can beat our Karate Master."

Claims like that didn't scare Ash. "Can I battle the Karate Master?" he asked eagerly.

"He's battling right now. In fact, he just accepted

a new challenger," said the Trainer. "But their battle should be over soon. The Karate Master is unbeatable."

Ash sighed. He didn't like to wait!

"Hey, Goh," Ash called across the drill grounds. "Let's go watch the battle!"

When Goh didn't respond, Ash walked in his friend's direction. The Fighting Dojo was in the middle of the city. Its outdoor drill grounds were in the center of the complex, divided into four sections. They were big enough for a hundred Hitmonlee to practice their bouncy high kicks on one field while a hundred Hitmonchan went through their exacting punching sequences on another. The grounds were

surrounded on all sides by walls and low buildings with ceramic-tiled roofs. The classic building style of clay with wood trim was a good match for the ancient teachings of karate.

"Hey, Goh!" Ash called out as he approached. "Still can't decide between Hitmonlee and Hitmonchan, right?"

It was a real quandary. Goh studied his Rotom Phone. He had no idea how he would choose just one. "Do I go for Hitmonchan with its razor-sharp punches . . ." Goh wondered out loud, "or Hitmonlee with its incredibly powerful kicks?" He was in agony, mesmerized by both Pokémon! "Do I really have

to decide on only one?" Goh asked the black-belt Trainer.

"Yes, that's the rule, Goh," the Trainer explained. "The Fighting Dojo can give you either a Hitmonlee or a Hitmonchan, but we can't give you both. You must choose one."

Then Goh had a brilliant idea. "I know, Ash! Let's each choose one, and afterward, you can trade yours for one of my other Pokémon!"

Ash wasn't necessarily on board with that plan, but before he had to respond, his Rotom Phone voiced an exciting alert: "There is a Pokémon World Coronation Series Trainer nearby."

"Pika?"

"Riol!"

Pikachu and Riolu were as curious about the notification as Ash. Where was the Trainer who was taking part in the tournament series?

The dojo Trainer looked around. "That would have to be the challenger who is battling the Karate Master." He motioned to a building with an impressive entrance, its tall, dark wooden doors closed.

Now Ash was even more interested in watching that matchup!

"Here we go!" he said, climbing the steps to the training room. At his sides, Pikachu and Riolu added their agreement. The team was ready! As Ash approached the doors, he prepared to introduce himself and declare his plans for a World Coronation Series battle.

But when Ash slid open the giant doors, something smashed into his face! He fell backward and hit the ground with a thud.

Goh rushed to his friend's side. "Ash, are you all right?" he asked with concern. His friend had been nearly flattened by a Hitmonchan. The Punching Pokémon was out cold on top of Ash.

Raboot took a fighting pose as it tried to figure out just what had happened. The Sobble on Goh's shoulder was so upset, it whimpered and used its water-based camouflage to disappear. Goh looked around and realized that the Hitmonchan had been defeated in battle.

Everyone in the training room appeared to be in shock—all except one Trainer across the room, who wore a black-and-orange bandana and a single battling glove.

A brawny, fit Trainer approached the Hitmonchan. "I guess that ends it," he grumbled, his face crumpled with distress. He was the dojo's Karate Master.

"All right," said the Trainer with the bandana. Her voice was stern and steady. "Referee, result?"

"Uh, right!" the referee said, still staring at the Karate Master and his fallen Pokémon. "The win goes to Grapploct! Which means the victor is Bea!"

"Are you all right, Hitmonchan?" Ash asked, lifting the Pokémon's head from the floor.

"Hitmonchan, you battled very well," the Karate Master said, kneeling down. "Now return."

On the sidelines, the black-belt Trainers who had watched the entire match were in awe. "Our Karate Master was barely able to land a single attack," said one.

"That Grapploct's scary," another Trainer admitted. "Its Trainer didn't give the Master a single opening. What a perfect showing."

"A Grapploct?" Ash repeated, full of curiosity.

"Pika?" Pikachu shared Ash's interest.

"Grapploct, return," said Bea, the winning Trainer. Her voice was still steady, and she did not look like she had just battled a Karate Master. Her fitted jersey and shorts were not at all dirty or wrinkled, and her knee pads were still a stark white. Most of all, her pale blue eyes were steely and unemotional.

"It was a good battle," Bea said to the Karate Master with a small but respectful bow. "I thank you."

Then the familiar buzz of a Rotom Phone vibrated in the training room of the Fighting Dojo.

"Is that from the World Coronation Series?" the Karate Master wondered aloud.

"A battle challenge has been issued," Bea's phone declared.

"You're registered with the World Coronation Series, right?" Ash inquired, looking right at her. He stepped forward to the threshold of the training room.

Bea's phone followed up with a prompt. "Do you wish to accept or reject it?"

CHAPTER SEVEN

"**M**y name is Ash Ketchum, and I'm a challenger in the World Coronation Series, too. Will you battle me?" Ash asked.

"I accept your challenge," Bea said.

"Really? All right!" Ash cried. Pikachu and Riolu were excited for a new match, too.

"An official battle has been registered," came the announcement from both Ash's and Bea's Rotom Phones.

"All right," she said. "My name is Bea. I come from the Galar region."

"Galar?!" Ash wondered aloud. After all, it was the home region of the reigning World Coronation Series Monarch Leon!

"Will you allow us to battle here?" Bea asked the Karate Master.

"Of course," he replied. "I don't mind at all." Turning to Ash, the Karate Master asked, "And your name? You said it's Ash? I am the master of this Fighting Dojo. Feel free to use this dojo as long as you want." After Ash thanked him gratefully, the Karate Master looked to Goh. "Are you here for a battle, too?"

Goh shook his head. "I heard if I came, I'd be able to receive either a Hitmonchan or a Hitmonlee, right?"

"Mm-hmm. You are correct. But that will happen only after you have defeated me in battle."

"I've got to battle you first?" Goh asked, utterly bewildered by this news.

"That is correct. But first we observe the battle between Ash and Bea." He took a deep breath. "Living alongside Pokémon . . . Battling together with Pokémon . . . That is what we strive for. Always." The Karate Master spoke the words like a mantra—like they were the idea that all the dojo Trainers believed at their very core.

The Karate Master began his introduction of the opponents. "Bea is a Gym Leader from the Galar region," he said. "And because her Gym specializes in Fighting-type Pokémon, that means she is an expert! The inheritor of Galar karate's hundred-year history.

In addition, she's been traveling the world, visiting every dojo, challenging them, and building up both her Pokémon and herself, seeking to reach perfection."

"She's ranked higher than you are," Goh said, showing Ash the screen on his Rotom Phone.

"Seven hundred and fifty-one," Ash murmured. Then he took off his shoes and walked toward the indoor pitch. The perimeter of the battle area was painted on the wooden floor. "I'm in the Great Class, too," Ash announced to Bea. "I rank eight hundred ninety. So far, we've won every battle we've been in. And Riolu's been trying especially hard."

"*Pikachu,*" Ash's Pokémon partner agreed.

"I sense an overflow of fighting spirit," the Karate

Master said with admiration. He stood with Goh, observing from near the doors. "You've raised your Pokémon well."

Ash appreciated the compliment. "Yeah, you can tell?" he asked over his shoulder. "A Master would, right?"

"Hey, Ash," Goh spoke out to his friend, "wouldn't it be good not to get carried away with yourself? Don't forget, she's ranked higher than you!"

"You worry too much," Ash responded. "We beat Korrina a while back, and she's a Fighting-type Gym Leader, too, right?"

"Korrina?" Bea repeated.

"Do you know Korrina, too?"

"Yes, we battled previously," Bea answered. "She was overconfident. I defeated her."

"Whaddaya mean, overconfident?" Ash asked. Pikachu and Riolu looked up at Ash, questioning.

"There is no need for further discussion," Bea stated.

Ash clenched his fists. He thought of his good-natured friend Korrina, with her bright smile and friendly greetings to his Pokémon—and how she and her Lucario had achieved Mega Evolution. One thing was for sure: Bea was nothing like Korrina.

"Why are you here?" Bea demanded. It sounded like she was accusing him of something.

"I want to get stronger, along with my Pokémon! If

I keep raising my rank, I'll be able to battle Leon," Ash answered honestly.

"I see," Bea said. "Every Trainer's biggest dream is to be able to defeat Leon. I wish to defeat him, too, and be recognized as the greatest in the world. That's why I'm competing."

"Well, *I'm* going to be the best!" Ash blurted, sure of himself and his Pokémon. "We're going to be the ones who beat Leon!"

"Then let's give it all we've got!" Bea declared.

Goh called out to his friend. "Don't get ahead of yourself! You'll win if you let Ash be Ash."

"Yeah, you just leave that to me!" Ash replied, looking back at his friend. He was pumped up! "Pikachu, Riolu, let's do this!"

In flew a Drone Rotom to begin the match protocol. It announced the two competitors and told them that they could each have two Pokémon in the battle. After asking Ash and Bea to bring out their Pokémon, the drone counted down. "Three . . . two . . . one . . . Go!"

"Now . . . Hawlucha, let's go!" Bea cried.

"Now, Farfetch'd, let's go!" Ash cried a split second later.

At once, Goh asked his Rotom Phone to give the details

on Bea's first choice for the battle. He, the Karate Master, and the other Trainers had moved to the middle of the sidelines, where there was a better view of the battle.

"Hawlucha," began Goh's phone. "The Wrestling Pokémon. A Fighting and Flying type. Using its wings, Hawlucha can control its position in the air. It overpowers opponents with lightning-fast moves."

Bea's Pokémon had colorful markings—tropical green feathers on the underside of its wide wings, red on its chest, and a bright orange crest.

"Hawlucha, huh?" Ash murmured under his breath as he developed a battle plan. He advised his Galarian Farfetch'd, "Be careful when Hawlucha is in midair, all right?"

"Faaar!" Farfetch'd agreed.

Ash had caught the regional Farfetch'd when he and Goh had been visiting Galar, right after Ash had decided to become part of the World Coronation Series. It had not taken long for Ash to realize that Galarian Farfetch'd was a valiant fighter, but he and Farfetch'd were still learning about being a team.

Just a moment later, the Drone Rotom declared that the battle had begun.

"Hone Claws, let's go!" Bea directed, and Hawlucha twisted up into the air, landing in a battle-ready pose after the attack-boosting move.

"Now, Farfetch'd, use Night Slash!" Ash called on

a damage-dealing move. Farfetch'd wielded his leek and sea-green energy pulsed toward Hawlucha.

Hawlucha took off into the air and easily dodged the pulses. Then it actually flew down onto the green end of Farfetch'd's leek! It stuck its landing on the leek like a world-class gymnast on a beam.

"Such balance!" Goh blurted in awe.

"Use Karate Chop!" Bea made her own chopping motions as she called the command. Hawlucha ran along the leek, right toward Farfetch'd, then swiftly slammed its opponent with a forceful chop.

The onslaught from Hawlucha surprised Farfetch'd, knocking the Wild Duck Pokémon down.

"Farfetch'd, no!" cried Ash.

"Flying Press, let's go!" Bea directed, and Hawlucha took off again, swooping toward Farfetch'd.

"Farfetch'd, get your leek!" Ash called, knowing it was the key to the Pokémon's most aggressive moves.

Farfetch'd scrambled across the pitch, snatching up the leek. It raised its long, yellow beak, proving to Ash that it was ready for its next move.

"All right! Good going, Farfetch'd" Ash yelled. "Now attack using Brutal Swing!"

Hawlucha came running at Farfetch'd, its wings spread wide. It made impact with the leek and grabbed ahold.

Farfetch'd began to swing its leek around in a circle, fast and tight. Hawlucha held on.

"Keep it spinning," Ash encouraged. Farfetch'd swung with all its might, but Hawlucha would not let go. They both were getting dizzy.

Bea saw a chance to gain an advantage. "Let's finish this," she said to Hawlucha. "Flying Press, let's go!"

Bea's call snapped Hawlucha to attention. It let go of the leek and flew up into the air.

Farfetch'd slowly came to a stop, its head still

whirling. It could barely hold on to its leek. It teetered from side to side.

"Look up!" Ash yelled, realizing Farfetch'd had lost track of Hawlucha. But it was too late.

Hawlucha was diving straight down, a blur of red and green. It landed on Farfetch'd with all its force. Farfetch'd fell flat on the floor with a crash, and its leek flew clear across the room.

Ash's friends looked on with concern. There was a big cloud of dust at the site of impact. It wasn't long before Drone Rotom announced that Farfetch'd was unable to battle.

"No way," Ash said, stunned. He pulled out a Poké Ball and asked Farfetch'd to return. He assured the Fighting-

type Pokémon that it had battled really hard. Ash's fist was shaking. "That won't happen again," he insisted.

"It looks like Ash has allowed the Gym Leader to get inside his head," the Karate Master said as a warning.

He, Goh, and the other Trainers were all sitting on their knees with their heels tucked under them. They could see that Bea was as calm as she'd been at the start of the match. Ash was less so.

Bea held out a Poké Ball and had Hawlucha return.

Goh gasped. Why would Bea call Hawlucha back when it still had so much fight left?

"What's next?" Ash wondered aloud. How would Bea follow a performance like the one from her feathered fighter?

CHAPTER EIGHT

Bea called for Grapploct. As soon as it appeared, the large Pokémon stretched out its mighty tentacles.

"There it is . . ." Ash whispered.

"Pika," Pikachu murmured with concern.

Goh's Rotom Phone shared the specifics of Ash's newest opponent. "Grapploct. The Jujitsu Pokémon. A Fighting type. Grapploct's entire body is made of overlapping muscles. Its tentacles have terrifying power for squeezing attacks."

Grapploct was enormous and blue with neon yellow spots. It stood on four of its suckered tentacles, and it waved the other four out to the sides, taunting its opponent.

"Isn't that the Pokémon you were battling against when we first came in?" Goh asked the Master.

"Yes," the Karate Master replied. "Neither my Hitmonlee nor my Hitmonchan stood a fighting chance against its strength."

Pikachu sized up Bea's next Pokémon. Pikachu took a strong, determined stance next to Ash. It was on all four legs with its tail up in battle position. *"Pikachu!"* it cried.

But Riolu had another idea about who would be next to battle. It stepped forward to its Trainer.

"Riolu?" Ash said. "You wanna jump in there?"

The young Fighting-type Pokémon had a real appetite for the fighting ring . . . or mat . . . or wherever a battle could be fought. "All right, Riolu. I choose you!"

Riolu flipped onto the battlefield.

"Pikachu, let's cheer for Riolu!" Ash said to his partner.

"Pika!" Pikachu agreed.

In the center of the Fighting Dojo floor, the two Pokémon were in an intense stare down.

"Grapplo, grapplo." Grapploct motioned with two tentacles. It was reaching out to Riolu—it seemed to be teasing the smaller Pokémon.

"Battle restart!" the Drone Rotom announced, and Ash was the first to make a move.

"Vacuum Wave!" he called to Riolu. In an instant, Riolu had shot off three pulses of the move.

"Use Detect! Now!" Bea countered. It was an odd decision because Detect was a move that did

not cause any damage. Detect would protect the Pokémon that used it from the effects of all the moves made that turn.

Grapploct swooshed through the air, and with each swoosh of its eight tentacles, it avoided Riolu's Vacuum Wave.

Then Bea came right back with Close Combat, and Grapploct dove toward Riolu.

"Double Team!" Ash called out. At once, Riolu made the move, creating copies of itself. *Pop! Pop! Pop! Pop!* The copies of Riolu popped up all around Grapploct. *Pop! Pop! Pop!*

The Jujitsu Pokémon didn't know which Riolu to

attack! It swatted at all the Riolus, but didn't land a single punch.

"Use Liquidation!" Bea said, sounding confident.

Grapploct aimed powerful streams of water at all the Riolus. As soon as the water made contact, the copies disappeared. Now Grapploct knew where to focus its energy.

"Riolu, keep it away!" Ash cried.

Riolu tried to deflect the water with its aerial kicks, but there were just too many blasts! Riolu skidded to a stop not far from Ash.

"That was what defeated both my Hitmonlee and Hitmonchan," the Karate Master told Goh.

"Riolu, you okay?" Ash asked with concern. The

Pokémon was struggling, but it had fortitude—it was strong, both in its fighting moves and its willingness to keep going, even when things were tough. Some people might say Riolu had grit because it signaled that it was still able to battle.

"Yes!" Ash cheered.

Meanwhile, Grapploct was massive and menacing. It had moved forward so it loomed directly over Riolu.

"I can't tell where it's going next!" Ash said. "What'll I do?" His usual battling instincts were not kicking in. Grapploct's strength and variety of attacks had thrown Ash off his game. Just watching Grapploct stare down at Riolu made Ash anxious. "We'd better wrap this thing up. It's now or never!" Ash yelled. "Charge in with Force Palm!"

On the sidelines, the Karate Master questioned Ash's rash decision. "Grappling's a bad move!" he said. After all, Grapploct was the Jujitsu Pokémon, and jujitsu was a style of martial arts that used special holds, throws, and blows.

Goh nodded. If Riolu got close enough, Grapploct could use its jujitsu and wrestling moves. Why would Ash play to his opponent's strengths?

Riolu ran in toward Grapploct, but Grapploct pulled

in its tentacles out of Riolu's reach. The Emanation Pokémon avoided Grapploct's trap, but could not land a move. Riolu flipped off Grapploct and landed, panting.

"*Rio, rio.*" Riolu tried to catch its breath.

"Head's up, Riolu!" Ash warned.

Grapploct looked confident. "*Grap-plah-plah-loct.*"

Ash was worried. "How do I get out of this?" he wondered out loud. "Riolu can't get close with all of those tentacles." Riolu was still panting, not yet ready for another move.

"This isn't looking good for Ash," Goh admitted.

"That attack was just what Grapploct wanted," the Karate Master agreed.

CHAPTER NINE

Ash surveyed the dojo, looking for a fresh approach. He needed a quick fix. He didn't know how long his young Fighting type could keep it up—as soon as Riolu got anywhere close to Grapploct, one of the Jujitsu Pokémon's blue tentacles would try to wrap around Riolu.

Now Riolu stared down its powerful opponent, panting. Riolu's shoulders rose up and down with each of its short breaths.

After considering all the possibilities, Ash made a decision. "All right, let's do it this way, Riolu!" he yelled. "Use Force Palm, and aim it right at the floor!"

Riolu leaped into the air. When it came down, it targeted one paw at the floor. The move sent a shock

wave across the wooden floor, right at Grapploct. Grapploct flailed its arms, trying to deflect the hit.

The Karate Master was baffled. "What's this?"

"It's Ash," Goh explained, "thinking outside the box." Goh had always admired Ash's ability to twist and spin common moves in uncommon ways.

"Riolu, use Force Palm again!" Ash called.

With fresh confidence, Riolu charged Grapploct.

Grapploct was ready. It wrapped one tentacle around Riolu, stopping it in its tracks.

"Octolock!" Bea commanded.

Before Riolu could use Force Palm, Grapploct put Octolock into play. It grabbed Riolu with first one tentacle, then more tentacles. Then it pushed Riolu to the ground and began to wrap it up in a tight tentacle squeeze.

"That's Octolock?" Ash asked, bewildered. Riolu squirmed around, kicking its legs.

"Pika?"

"Ash's strategy didn't work," Goh said. "That's a pinning move, right?"

"It's fallen into the trap," the Karate Master observed.

"Riolu, you gotta hang on!" Ash encouraged. "Get out of there! Use Vacuum Wave!"

Riolu tried to whirl its fists, but it couldn't move!

"Pity," Bea stated, feeling very sure of herself. "You make lots of useless moves."

"Riolu, you've got to kick the ground with your legs!" Ash cried, trying to help Riolu manage an escape.

When Riolu pounded both legs against the ground, the energy launched both Riolu and Grapploct into the air. When they landed, Grapploct lost hold of the smaller Pokémon. Riolu tumbled across the wooden floor. It was free! It panted as it forced itself to stand.

All the spectators were impressed with Riolu's maneuvers, but the battle was far from won.

"Awesome!" Ash called. "Riolu, hang in there!"

"Use Liquidation!" Bea commanded as soon as Grapploct was up in its battle pose. At once, a powerful force of water was at the Jujitsu Pokémon's command.

"Use Reversal!" Ash directed.

"Rioooooo!" Riolu opened its paws wide and called on its inner energy.

Goh was shocked by this move.

"There, that's Reversal," the Karate Master said. "The more you've exhausted your strength, the more damage it's going to deliver! It's sink or swim!"

"Rioluuuuu!" Riolu was still standing with its paws stretched out, channeling its strength.

Grapploct leaped into the air.

Riolu leaped into the air.

Then their two moves met in the air. All that power, all at once! The moves were so powerful they canceled each other out!

As soon as they landed, Bea directed, "One more time! Octolock!"

Grapploct slithered across the floor, headed for Riolu. With one smooth pouncing motion, Grapploct had Riolu trapped in Octolock again.

"Riolu, no!" Ash cried.

Riolu squirmed in pain as Grapploct's hold became tighter, tighter, tighter.

"Oh no!" the Karate Master exclaimed.

"Surrender while you can," Bea demanded. "Or I will have to force you to surrender!"

"We haven't given up yet!" Ash insisted. "We broke out of this move once before. Just hang in there!"

"Have it your way," Bea stated, taking her stance. "Liquidation. Let's go!"

Grapploct had so many high-level moves! And Bea was using Liquidation's full-force blast of water now? With Riolu in such close range?

"Riolu!" Ash yelled with concern.

"Pika!" Pikachu called out.

Grapploct's tentacle took aim and released. The blast tossed Riolu across the dojo. This time, Riolu did not get up.

Drone Rotom buzzed in and hovered above Riolu. "Riolu's unable to battle," said Drone Rotom, "which means the victory goes to Bea!"

"I thank you for the match," Bea said, without any excitement at all. She and Grapploct both gave polite bows.

"You all right?" Ash asked, rushing to Riolu's side.

"Pika." Pikachu looked from Riolu to Ash.

Like Bea, Drone Rotom also did not show any emotion toward Ash and his defeated Pokémon. It continued with its summary of the match. "As a result of today's battle, there has been a change in the World Coronation Series ranking, effective immediately!" Drone Rotom usually had such a

pleasant chirp as it went about its duties, but today, it sounded a little short, and possibly smug.

"Bea won an overwhelming victory," Goh said, still in shock. "It looks like none of Ash's out-of-the-box moves or speed attacks seemed to have any effect on her at all." Goh was not used to this. He was used to congratulating Ash after a match, swapping high fives, and planning their next adventure.

The Karate Master shook his head. "Hawlucha and Grapploct didn't take much damage, either." His observation was a certain sign of an uneven battle. Bea and her Pokémon were at the top of their game.

"That's it. I lost it." Ash sat with Riolu in his arms. He had been on a winning streak for so long. It was an

unfamiliar feeling, being on the losing end. His phone showed his ranking change right before his eyes. He dropped from 890 to 930.

"Pika."

"Wow. She was a tough opponent," Goh said. "Wasn't she, Ash?" But Ash didn't respond.

"Now, Grapploct, return," said Bea. The Gym Leader from Galar turned to the Karate Master. "I shall take leave of you at this point. Thank you very much for letting us use your dojo." Then she walked past Ash, his Pokémon, and his friend without saying a thing. The match was truly over, and Ash had truly lost his first World Coronation Series battle.

The Karate Master turned to Goh with fresh

energy. "Now, young Goh," he said, "I believe that it's our turn."

Goh was caught off guard.

"You will get your choice of Pokémon to add to your team, but only after you've beaten me!" the Karate Master reminded him.

"You mean right now?" Goh couldn't believe it. Just watching Ash's grueling duel had been exhausting enough. How would he manage to battle the Karate Master now?

Luckily, Raboot was determined enough for the two of them.

And if anything could distract Goh from the shock of Ash's loss, it was the chance to acquire a brand-new Pokémon for his collection!

Later that day, everyone was still trying to process what had gone down at the dojo. "At least you won your match," Ash said to Goh.

Goh nodded and looked over at the newest member of his team. "And I chose Hitmonchan!" The Punching Pokémon made several practice jabs by his side.

Ash crouched down to talk to his Pokémon. They had battled so valiantly that day. "Riolu? Farfetch'd? Sorry, guys. We got beat—though we trained really hard."

"Rio-lu."

"Farrrr-fetch'd."

The two Pokémon responded to Ash with affection and understanding.

"Pika." Pikachu's tone suggested more concern. After all, Pikachu had known Ash for a much longer time.

"I've never had a battle like that before. But next time won't be the same!" Ash said with determination. "Bea's gonna find out just how good we are!"

It had been Ash's first setback on his mission to face the Monarch, Leon, again. Suffering such a bitter loss made an epic battle with Leon feel like a distant dream.

But now Ash had a new, more immediate goal: He wanted a rematch with Bea. It was his next mission. He wanted to prove that he and his Pokémon were strong enough to face the Gym Leader from Galar again. It would take a lot of training, but that didn't mean he wouldn't keep signing up for World Coronation Series battles along the way!

CHAPTER TEN

The loss to Bea was hard. Afterward, the match played over and over in Ash's mind. He had visions of Farfetch'd, still woozy from Brutal Swing, looking up just in time for Hawlucha to slam him into the floor. That memory was not a good one.

Even so, Riolu's battle with Grapploct haunted Ash even more. It seemed like there was no chance that Riolu ever could have won against the blue behemoth. The more Ash thought about it, the more he believed that he should never have let Riolu get so close to the other Pokémon. If Riolu had avoided the Octolock, they would have had a chance.

Ash had such faith in Riolu. Ever since Riolu was still in its Egg, Ash had been drawn to its intense aura—and vice versa. Riolu yearned to battle like no

Pokémon Ash had ever known. Fresh from its cracked
Egg, Riolu had wanted to figure things out on its own.
Riolu had been full of mistrust at first and had run out
into the wild all on its own. Luckily, Ash and Pikachu
had followed Riolu. When they found the newly
hatched Pokémon, Riolu was exchanging blows with
an angry Onix, and the Onix had the upper hand in the
battle (even though an Onix has no hands!).

Riolu had watched in awe as Ash and Pikachu
brought down the gigantic Onix with one well-placed
Iron Tail move. Maybe that was the moment that Riolu
had realized it might be good to be part of a team.

Immediately after, Riolu had tackled Pikachu and

looked Ash in the eye. *"Olu, olu, olu. Oir, oir,"* Riolu had said. It was insistent. It was determined.

"Do you want to get stronger?" Ash had asked. "If that's what you want, then help me out!"

Just then, the Onix reared up its rocky head again. With direction from Ash, Riolu used Vacuum Wave and other moves to defeat the Onix. It was a big moment.

"Riolu, that was awesome," Ash said, kneeling down to talk to the baby Fighting type. "Your battling was really something else."

"Pika, pika!" Pikachu wanted Riolu to know that it agreed!

But Riolu was still so young. It had used all its energy in the battle.

"You're beat," Ash realized. Then the Trainer bent down and offered to give Riolu a piggyback ride to the Pokémon Center. Both Ash and Pikachu were surprised when Riolu refused. The baby Pokémon wanted to walk on its own.

"You're pretty stubborn, aren't you?" Ash said with a laugh.

Riolu was wise beyond its years. Ash had started using Riolu in World Coronation Series matchups almost immediately. And the wins had kept coming. So Ash was especially rocked by their first tournament defeat.

From that point on, Ash tried to develop battle plans for Riolu—plans that would keep the young Fighting type far from its opponent. As before, Ash was always ready for a new battle. He wanted to put their new plan to a test. The outcome, however, was not good. Ash and Riolu could not find a rhythm. Riolu was not effective from a distance. The young Pokémon could not overcome its own instincts, which told it to battle up close, to take its most powerful moves right to the opposing Pokémon.

What was worse was that it wasn't just the loss to Bea's incredibly well-trained Pokémon that upset Ash. He also did not like losing to Bea. Ash did not understand her. She was so serious, and she did not seem to enjoy battling—or even winning.

Ash did not get to enjoy winning either, not for some time. He and Riolu had three straight losses. Ash fell out of the Great Class. It was a slump, a rut, and, in Ash's mind, a tragedy. But it's hard to keep a good Trainer—and his good Pokémon—down.

CHAPTER ELEVEN

Zap! Blast! Zap!

In a clearing not far from Professor Cerise's lab, there was all kinds of battling action! "Riolu, use Vacuum Wave!" Ash directed.

Riolu whirled its fists and sent pulses of Vacuum Wave, one of its signature moves. Pikachu took zigzagging leaps to try to avoid the damage-dealing move. Riolu had improved the speed and accuracy of its move, and Pikachu had to bolt to escape.

"Force Palm!" yelled Ash.

Pikachu took its battle to the air with flips and grunts, and just as Riolu prepared to release a well-aimed Force Palm hit, Ash called it off. "That's enough!" he yelled. "Awesome! You got close at just the right time, didn't you?" he said to Riolu as he waved it over.

"Rio." Riolu had improved its strategy and was proud of its hard work.

"Pika." Pikachu trotted up to Ash.

"Ah, thanks a lot, buddy," Ash said.

"Pikachu."

Ash reached out and gave Pikachu a pat. Pikachu leaned in to Ash's hand, enjoying the show of affection. It felt good to be needed! The Pokémon gave a happy squeak.

Pikachu had been such a help with the increased training. It had been intense, and Ash knew that having Pikachu on his team made all the difference.

Ash had recently been reminded that he couldn't

take Pikachu's steadfast loyalty for granted. He had been super focused on training, especially on Riolu and Farfetch'd, since the two Fighting types were both new to his battling squad. With Ash working hard to get the most out of their moves, he had not been paying as much attention to Pikachu.

It had all come to a head when Ash's mom, Delia, was visiting. She spent a night in the spare room at Professor Cerise's home when she had been in town. She'd always been especially fond of Pikachu, since it was Ash's first-ever Pokémon. She could even remember when Ash and Pikachu were not such kindred spirits—when they first met, they did

not really get along! Now, during Delia's short stay, she showed Pikachu a special kindness, and it had even cuddled up and slept next to her in her bed, remembering the closeness of its early years with Ash.

After Delia had left early the next day, Ash went right back to training—that is, training Riolu and Farfetch'd. But Pikachu had had enough of being ignored! The Electric-type Pokémon made a rash move and decided to leave Professor Cerise's place without telling anyone and track Delia down. Luckily, Mimey followed Pikachu, more for protection than company. Pikachu was on a mission, and nothing was going to stop it.

That was a rude emotional awakening for Ash. When he discovered Pikachu was gone, he thought about . . . well, everything. He soon realized he had been wrong to neglect Pikachu. He had put too much emphasis on training, and he knew he had to make things right with Pikachu. Pikachu would always be his first Pokémon partner.

Ash's World Coronation Series journey had included many twists and turns, and a number of bumps and potholes, too. He had never imagined he would experience three straight losses. But he also never imagined that watching Goh defeat and capture

a Flygon would help him snap out of his slump.

Just at the point that Ash was most upset about his plummeting rank, Goh had insisted they investigate a strange sandstorm for Professor Cerise. Inside that sandstorm, they had found a number of peculiar Pokémon, including Trapinch, the Ant Pit Pokémon, and Vibrava, the Vibration Pokémon. Of course, Goh caught them both!

But it was Goh and Raboot's clever plan to catch the formidable Flygon that had really impressed Ash. Who would have thought to use a Draco Meteor to launch a Dodge move? When Goh explained that his unconventional strategy had been inspired by Ash's own out-of-the-box battle methods, Ash realized he just needed a fresh take on training. He had been playing it too safe—playing to not lose instead of playing to win.

Each Pokémon not only had the moves special to its type, but also had its own battle style. Just like Pikachu did not like to be trapped in a Poké Ball, Riolu did not like to have to battle from a distance. It took patience and dedication to *really* understand Pokémon. Ash had always known this, but he needed to be reminded from time to time.

Now Ash was trying to make training time fun! And he knew he needed to include all of his Pokémon, to help each one know that it had something important to offer the team. One way to do

that was to train together. There was nothing like a few one-on-one practice battles between friends!

"Next battle is Farfetch'd and Dragonite!" he announced. The other Pokémon had been spectators for Pikachu and Riolu's matchup. They were ready for their turn at improving their skills . . . and getting Ash's attention.

"*Far,*" Farfetch'd agreed, and Dragonite gave a friendly grunt.

A voice interrupted them. "Ash!" Soon Goh appeared in the clearing with Raboot at his side. Sobble balanced on Raboot's head as the Fire-type Pokémon skidded smoothly to a stop.

"Let's go to Johto!" Goh said. He gave Ash a knowing smile.

"Johto?" Ash repeated. What had prompted Goh's sudden interest in the region?

Goh held up his Rotom Phone as an answer. Right there, on Goh's screen, was a picture of Bea, with her mop of thick, silver, floppy hair. The very same Bea who had been the first Trainer to defeat Ash on his World Coronation Series journey. Looking closely at the screen, Ash could see that Bea had jumped up in the rankings. She was already at 193!

Of course, after falling to Bea, Ash had suffered other losses. He had dropped so low that he had fallen from the Great Class back to the Normal Class. Those losses had definitely taught Ash something, and he had been training hard and battling decisively ever since. After just a few of his new practice sessions including his whole team of Pokémon, Ash noticed that his Pokémon seemed more excited to battle. They were quicker, they listened better, and they were back to their winning ways! Ash felt it, too. They had upped their game, and they had made their way back to the Great Class!

But was he prepared for a rematch with Bea so soon?

CHAPTER TWELVE

Only a few hours later, the two friends and their Pokémon were on a small yacht bound for the Johto region, west of Kanto. It would be more rural in Johto, which meant fewer cities and more wooded areas. There was a fair amount of water as well. All this meant that Goh was eager to track down some new Pokémon for his collection.

"I've been hoping I could catch some Johto Pokémon!" Goh exclaimed from the bow of the boat. "We both want good results. No doubt about it!" Already, Goh had a fishing rod with some prime Pokémon bait on its hook! But he hadn't gotten any bites.

Ash had figured out that Bea was training at a Pokémon Gym in Cianwood City. And, Ash being Ash, he knew the Gym Leader at that particular training facility:

It was Chuck. The two had battled a while back. Ash recalled the Gym Leader's enthusiasm for Pokémon training. He remembered that Chuck's Pokémon were strong and steady, always maintaining a sense of calm.

But Ash did not have plans to battle Chuck today. His goal was to rematch with Bea.

As they approached the Gym, Ash was starting to feel anxious. Goh, however, was pouting. He had not caught any Pokémon from the boat. Sobble tried to comfort him, petting Goh's dark hair with its webbed foot. Still, Goh kept sulking. He vowed there was no way he would leave Johto without catching at least one new Pokémon!

The Gym was a large, noble-looking building. It was

newer than the Fighting Dojo in Saffron City, and it was set back from the street. Ash ran along a long stone walkway to the front doors. He swung them open and saw a practice battle in progress. It was Chuck and Bea!

Their Poliwrath and Grapploct were sparring.

"Impressive!" Gym Leader Chuck said with admiration, calling all the way across the Gym's battling field. "But perhaps I should have known you'd withstand Poliwrath's Poison Jab."

Before Bea could reply, there was the vibration of a Rotom Phone.

"Oh, could that be a message from the World Coronation Series?" Chuck wondered aloud.

"Let's battle, Bea!" Ash declared from the doorway. Ash and his friends entered the Gym training room, but Bea didn't say a thing.

"Wait, I think I remember this young man . . ." said Chuck.

Both Ash's and Bea's phones announced the battle challenge at once.

"A battle challenge has been issued," the Rotom Phones said. "Do you wish to accept or reject it?"

"Cool! I wanna have a rematch right now!" Ash said with enthusiasm.

Bea did not respond immediately. She looked at Ash like she didn't know who he was.

"Uh, don't you remember me, or the battle we had?" Ash asked. He couldn't believe Bea didn't remember him. Here he was, wearing his usual long shorts, sky-blue vest, green backpack, and red cap. He looked exactly the same!

"The Riolu Trainer," Bea responded at last.

"Pika?" Pikachu was just as surprised.

"Maybe she just doesn't remember your name," Goh suggested. Ash didn't think that made things any better. He'd been working toward this rematch for weeks!

"Have you battled against this young man before,

young lady?" Chuck asked, walking over to Bea.

"I remember Riolu and Farfetch'd," Bea admitted.

The Gym Leader threw his head back and laughed out loud. His long, bushy mustache shook when he laughed. "That sounds like something you would say!"

"If this is a challenge, I accept," said Bea. She was all business, just like the last time.

It struck Ash as funny that Chuck would refer to Bea as "young lady." When they'd met before, Bea was so confident, so skilled. Ash had not realized that Bea might not be that much older than he was.

A moment later, both Ash's and Bea's phones

noted that an official battle had been registered.

"All right!" The moment Ash had been preparing for was here at last.

"Pika!" Pikachu jumped onto Ash's shoulder, looking up for the challenge.

Riolu gave a low growl from where it stood by Ash's side.

"Grapploct, return for now," Bea said to her big, blue, octopus-like Fighting type. Even as it returned to its Poké Ball, its long arms never stopped moving.

"Chuck, is it okay if we have our battle in your Gym?" Ash asked.

"Ah, Ash. I thought that was you! Greetings!" the Gym Leader said.

"Hi! It's been a while!" Ash responded.

Pikachu gave a wave, too.

"Of course you can use my Gym! No holding back!"

"Thank you so much!" Ash said, always grateful for the generosity of Gym Leaders and others in the Pokémon community.

"You and he are acquainted?" Bea questioned. She seemed uncertain about this.

"I'm a Gym Leader!" Chuck answered, putting his hands on his hips. "People say my roaring fists do the talking! I never forget a Trainer I've crossed fists with!" He talked a big game and was a strong Gym Leader, but he also came off as a genuinely nice guy.

"Guess what, Bea? I was able to make it back into the Great Class," Ash told his opponent. Chances were good that Bea had not even realized that Ash had fallen down to the Normal Class. She seemed very focused on only her own progress.

"Oh, you had dropped down into the Normal Class?" Chuck said. "Of course, you have to be in the same class to have an official battle."

"Right!" Goh agreed, putting a reassuring hand on Ash's arm. Even though Goh wasn't participating in the World Coronation Series, he was up on all the rules for the competition. "This battle with Bea will be a rematch."

CHAPTER THIRTEEN

Ash and Bea headed to opposite ends of the battle area. Goh, Raboot, Sobble, Chuck, and Poliwrath took seats on the short bleachers on the sideline.

"Here's where I win and climb even higher!" Ash declared, feeling very sure of himself and his Pokémon.

At that moment, the group was joined by a Drone Rotom. The Drone Rotom announced that they were approved for a Great Class battle. *Great Class!* Ash felt great hearing that again! The Drone Rotom also told them that Ash and Bea would each be allowed two Pokémon.

"Pikachu, Riolu, stay on your toes!" Ash advised. The Pokémon had taken their places on either side of Ash.

When the Drone Rotom prompted them, Ash and Bea prepared their Pokémon and waited for the countdown.

"Three . . . two . . . one . . . go!"

Ash called on Pikachu.

Bea called on Hitmontop.

They were ready to battle!

"Hitmontop, wow!" As usual, Goh immediately called on his Rotom Phone for the details on Ash's opponent's Pokémon. "Hitmontop," Goh's phone began. "The Handstand Pokémon. A Fighting type. Hitmontop spins like a top as it battles, and centrifugal force adds ten times the destructive power to its attacks."

Hitmontop had come out of the Poké Ball already

whirling around on its head. Goh was excited to see how Bea's Pokémon would use its spinning power in the matchup. Of course, Goh was rooting for Ash as always, but he was also a student of Pokémon. He was always up for learning something new!

"Battle begin!" the Drone Rotom announced.

"Hitmontop, use Gyro Ball!" Bea directed. It didn't take long for Hitmontop to show off its spinning power. The speed was incredible!

"Pikachu, use Thunderbolt!" Ash called on one of his and Pikachu's favorite moves to start. Pikachu zapped Hitmontop, but the other Pokémon didn't slow down.

"Pikachu, get close!" Ash directed. "Use Iron Tail!"

Pikachu raced forward and then spun around, so its electrified tail made contact.

"Even so far," Goh said, noting that both Pokémon had made good hits.

"Pikachu, Quick Attack!" Ash called. Pikachu bounded forward and landed a Quick Attack, sending Hitmontop down the field. "All right, use Electroweb!" Ash said.

"Those are quick follow-ups!" Chuck observed.

"It looks like Ash is working on his 'win-it-through-speed' strategy," Goh said.

Pikachu prepared to cast Electroweb into the air.

"Slow it down," Ash advised, realizing that Hitmontop was only getting faster with the last few moves.

Ash watched as Pikachu's web zapped Hitmontop to a stop. The Pokémon was facedown on the floor.

"Well, that's the end of its speed game," Ash said.

"Focus Energy!" Bea directed.

"Be careful out there!" Ash warned his partner.

Taking in the action, Chuck noted to Goh, "Focus Energy will increase the chance for Hitmontop's attacks to do massive damage."

Bea observed Hitmontop closely. "Triple Kick! Let's go!"

With the boost from Focus Energy, Hitmontop charged.

Pikachu braced for impact. Triple Kick lived up to

its name, whamming Pikachu not one, not two, but three times.

"That had quite an effect!" Chuck stated the obvious.

"Ash tried to end it with Electroweb, but Hitmontop just shook it off," Goh said.

"Pikachu, are you all right?" Ash called to his favorite Electric type.

Pikachu struggled to all four paws, but readied itself for more battle.

"Okay, how about this one?" Ash said. "Use Electroweb! Aim it at the floor!"

Pikachu followed through with the move. It leaped straight up and then came straight down. Its electric tail sent jolts along the floor, creating a charged web. This new direction caught Bea and Hitmontop off guard!

"What? What's going on?!" Chuck questioned. He'd never seen anything quite like that on his Gym's floor.

"Gyro Ball!" Bea tried the reliable move.

Hitmontop spun at a surprising speed, bouncing off the electric threads of the web. It ricocheted back and forth, like it was trapped in a pinball machine.

"Use Iron Tail!" Ash yelled, and Pikachu hopped over the web threads to make contact with Hitmontop.

"Now Quick Attack!" said Ash.

Pikachu had barely landed when it bolted back into the air for Quick Attack. This move would be the last of the matchup.

Hitmontop fell to the floor. It was stunned.

The Drone Rotom buzzed onto the Gym floor to confirm that Hitmontop was unable to battle.

"Yes! We just got our first win!" Ash cried after the Drone Rotom made its announcement. "Good going, Pikachu!"

Pikachu turned around and gave Ash a smile. Then it gave itself a good shake, sweat flying from its coat. *"Pikachu!"*

"They won! Ash and Pikachu, you did great!" Goh

encouraged his friends, clenching his fists in support.

"Sobble!" Goh's Water-type Pokémon added a happy cheer.

"Getting interesting, isn't it?" Chuck said, thoroughly enjoying himself.

"Ash wasn't able to take down even one of Bea's Pokémon the last time," Goh shared with Chuck. "If he can keep going like he is now . . ."

"But the real question is, what does the young lady think of her Pokémon's defeat?" Chuck pointed out.

Goh nodded. Chuck made a good point. How *would* Bea respond? Goh had a feeling that Chuck understood Bea far better than either he or Ash did.

CHAPTER FOURTEEN

"**A**ll right, Hitmontop, return," Bea said. "You battled very well." She placed the Poké Ball in her pocket and slipped out another. Without a pause, she threw the Poké Ball into battle. "Now go! Grapploct!"

Grapploct appeared with the same menacing expression as before. Its arms were still outstretched, ready to grasp its next victim.

"All right. Grapploct's up next," Ash commented.

"Riiiiiiiii," Riolu growled.

"Pikachu, can you stay in there?" Ash observed the Electric type's reaction. The extended use of Electroweb had been an exhausting effort, but when Pikachu got on all four legs and squinted its eyes, staring at Grapploct, Ash had his answer.

Riolu cheered for its teammate.

Goh was shocked that Ash chose to keep Pikachu in against the massive Jujitsu Pokémon. Raboot and Sobble also seemed concerned.

"Use Quick Attack!" called Ash, and Pikachu raced ahead.

"Close Combat!" Bea called.

As Pikachu drew near, Grapploct hopped over the tiny Electric type. When Pikachu turned around, Grapploct flung it across the Gym with one swipe of a tentacle. Then it kept up with its Close Combat moves, batting Pikachu back and forth, bashing it on one side and then the other. It was quite a beating.

As soon as Pikachu could escape, Ash called for Thunderbolt. Pikachu sent a jolt of electricity at the giant Fighting type . . . and got giant results. The whole battlefield lit up! Grapploct tumbled back, making impact with the ground. When the smoky cloud cleared, energy pulses were still fizzing around Grapploct's body.

"It's still up," Ash said with wonder.

"Use Octolock!" Bea instructed, and Grapploct stalked forward.

"Iron Tail!" Ash yelled. Pikachu jumped up, bouncing from tentacle to tentacle on Grapploct, searching for a good angle.

But then Grapploct made its Octolock move. Pikachu was caught in its squeeze.

"Pikachu, no!" Ash cried. Pikachu squirmed against

Grapploct's arms. "Don't struggle against it!" Ash yelled. "It'll only get tighter!" Ash watched as Pikachu strained. "All right, then . . . Pikachu, Thunderbolt!"

Pikachu tried to make the move, but just couldn't pull it off in this stifling grip of Grapploct. Thunderbolt fizzled out.

"Pikachu can't make enough power," Ash said to himself. "All right," he called out, "this time, use Iron Tail!"

Unfortunately, the result was the same: no result at all.

"Neither Thunderbolt nor Iron Tail is working," Goh observed.

"That's the terrifying part about Octolock. Those tentacles can completely restrain an opponent!" Chuck explained.

"There's got to be a way out," Ash murmured. Next to him, Riolu was frustrated.

"Use Liquidation!" Bea directed. That was the same move she'd used to take down Riolu before.

Pikachu wailed as it was thrown across the Gym floor. *"Pikaaaa!"*

"Pikachu is unable to battle!" the Drone Rotom announced.

"Pikachu!" Ash yelled.

"Rio," Riolu said as it stepped onto the battlefield. Riolu bent down and lifted up the weary Pikachu, then carried its teammate on its back all the way back to Ash.

"Riolu, thanks," Ash said. Riolu turned carefully, so Ash could take Pikachu into his arms. Ash realized how much Riolu's relationship with Pikachu meant to the young Fighting type.

"Pikachu, thanks for everything," Ash said. Pikachu had put its all into that day's battles. "Now, why don't you cheer Riolu on?"

"Pi-ka-chu," the tired Pokémon agreed.

Ash turned to Riolu. "It's up to you," he said, and

Riolu made its way onto the battlefield again. Grapploct was waiting.

"Hey, I detect a heightened fighting spirit!" Chuck said from the sideline. He could feel the tension in the air.

"The last time those two battled, Riolu lost to Grapploct. The Octolock was just too much," Goh admitted.

"Okay, Riolu, go!" Ash said, and Riolu took off running—right at Grapploct.

"Use Liquidation!" Bea was starting with the same move that had finished off the battle with Pikachu.

Ash countered with Vacuum Wave. Riolu fired off its move before Grapploct could shoot Liquidation. The hit shocked Grapploct.

Riolu started to move in on its opponent. "Stay back for a bit," Ash advised.

"*Olu!*" Rio said with a grunt, bouncing backward.

"A preplanned strategy," Chuck said thoughtfully. "Vacuum Wave blew Liquidation's water away."

"But he's not moving to the next attack very fast," Goh observed.

"I get the feeling Ash is trying to break up the attack rhythm," Chuck told Goh.

Grapploct and Riolu faced each other without making a move.

"Hmm," Bea murmured after a while. Finally, she called, "Octolock!"

Grapploct bounded forward on its tentacles and pounced on Riolu. Riolu did not even try to evade the move.

"What?" asked Bea, astonished. "He's smiling."

It was true. Ash *was* smiling.

Grapploct wrapped its suckered arms around Riolu, turned the Emanation Pokémon around, and began to tighten its hold. Riolu didn't do a thing.

"Riolu's not trying to break free," Chuck realized.

"Must be a strategy," Goh commented. "But why?"

Everyone in the Gym watched with curiosity. What

did Ash and Riolu have planned? Could they overcome the sheer power of Octolock?

Riolu was in the very position Ash had dreaded in training: in Grapploct's grasp, caught in the Octolock! But Riolu had convinced Ash that it could take the close contact.

"That's it, Riolu. Get in sync with Grapploct's movements!" Ash called out. "That's how we break the Octolock." That revealed their strategy to everyone in the Pokémon Gym—but would it work?

"That sounds interesting to me," Bea admitted. Even she wondered how it all would turn out! "Let's see what you mean."

Sobble and Raboot were impressed with Ash and

Riolu's plan. "Bea's gonna let them do it!" said Goh, fascinated.

"Riolu, make sure you've built up enough power," Ash said, waiting for the right moment. Riolu closed its eyes and focused its energy. It tapped into the power it had inside.

"Use Force Palm!" Ash yelled.

Riolu's eyes popped open, and it spread its palm against Grapploct's tentacle. The shock wave broke Grapploct's grip, and Riolu bounded free!

"Pika!" Pikachu cheered from the sideline.

"All right!" yelled Ash.

"That was amazing!" Goh exclaimed. "It didn't put up a fight against the Octolock and waited until the last moment as Grapploct tightened its grip. Then it used Force Palm from the inside. Grapploct took a lot of damage, and Riolu broke free!"

Grapploct was struggling to pull itself up, but Riolu was already in its battle-ready pose.

"It appears your Force Palm move has become stronger," Bea said. "So we will answer you with all of the strength we possess!" Bea crossed her wrists over her chest and made karate moves. "Use Close Combat!" she called.

Close Combat was designed for dealing damage, and it didn't leave much power left for defense. Bea was putting it all on the battlefield!

"Here we go! Force Palm again!" Ash called to Riolu.

"Let's go!" Ash and Bea cried at the same time.

Both Pokémon launched into the air. They met above the battlefield and tumbled in midair as they grappled. Riolu was trying to complete Force Palm, and Grapploct was aiming for a Close Combat punch. At last, they both made contact, and there was a forceful blast that threw them both back to the Gym floor.

Everyone waited in silence. Both Pokémon lay flat on their backs.

The familiar hum of the Rotom Drone was a signal to the Trainers and spectators. "Both Grapploct and Riolu are unable to battle!" the Rotom Drone announced. "As such, this is judged to be a draw, with no change in the rankings!"

"It ended in a tie," Goh murmured in disbelief. Even after all of Ash's training and strategy, it was a draw.

Chuck broke out in laughter. "Now, *that* was a great battle!" he yelled. "My compliments to the Trainers and Pokémon alike!" He seemed proud just to have hosted such a well-played battle in his Gym. Standing up, he said, "Why don't we all take a break?"

After that battle, it seemed like a good idea.

CHAPTER FIFTEEN

Not much later, the Trainers, Pokémon, and their friends were looking at the most colorful and fancy desserts they had ever seen. There were cakes topped with berries, bars of every shade of the rainbow, cups of pudding and caramel, and chocolate of all kinds!

"So much! Awesome!" Ash exclaimed. Had he ever even imagined such an amazing spread of absolute deliciousness?

"This is my main energy source! The sweetest desserts you'll ever find! They power your body's engine. We even have some especially for the Pokémon!" Chuck was as excited about his tasty treats as he was about Pokémon battles! Ash had to wonder if that was why his belly was as mighty as his fists. A whole feast of desserts was not the typical menu for top Trainers. Many Pokémon Trainers ate like elite athletes, focusing on fresh foods and avoiding sugar.

"Who knew?" Goh said, taking special interest in the layered brownie.

"We can have any of these?" Ash asked.

"Of course! With the excellent battling skills you all demonstrated, please have as much as you like!" Chuck answered.

"Great! Let's eat!" No one had to tell Ash or Goh twice. They were in heaven! So were the Pokémon, who shared a platter of fine fruits and other snacks.

Then Ash wondered how Bea would feel about all the sweet stuff. She was so serious about her training!

It appeared that Chuck had been thinking the same thing. "Young lady?" he began, "perhaps this is not to your taste, so . . ." He held up a simple loaf of bread that looked a little more healthy.

But to everyone's surprise, Bea was devouring the brownies and fruit bars. There was even chocolate smeared on her face. "I really love it! It's delicious!" she said between bites. She gobbled up a key lime bar. All her Pokémon were holding treats in both hands as well.

"Whaddya know! She loves it!" Goh said with a laugh.

"Happy to hear it," Chuck said with a smile. He was as good a host at mealtime as he was at gametime.

"So, you do like sweet stuff?" Ash said. He felt like he was getting to know a lot more about Bea than during their first matchup.

"Oh, my, yes!" Bea licked her fingers with relish.

Pikachu hopped over and looked up at Bea, its head tilted with curiosity.

"Here," Bea said. She kneeled down and offered Pikachu a nibble. They both took a bite. "Tasty!" said Bea, smiling. "Riolu, would you like some as well?"

"Olu." Riolu seemed nervous.

"Grapploct." Grapploct came up from behind and nudged Riolu, insisting he give it a try.

"Here!" Bea said. Her voice was lighter, kinder.

Riolu took the bite in both paws. When it tasted the treat, pure delight spread across its face. Scrumptious!

"Way to go! Good for you both!" Ash said. It felt good, seeing Riolu making friends with other Pokémon and Trainers. It really had not been that long ago that Riolu had hatched from that Egg. The young Pokémon had been so headstrong, so full of mistrust. Riolu had matured so much—and not only in his battling skills.

"The way you broke the Octolock was impressive," Bea said to Ash.

"I tell you, winning battles isn't so easy," Ash admitted. "I'm gonna train much harder!"

"Mark my words, I *will* proceed on to the Ultra Class," Bea replied, suddenly serious again.

"I'll be moving up with you!" Ash assured Bea.

Chuck released a deep belly laugh once again. "Just as expected!" he said. "Young lady, you accept your opponent's strength while reaching for your own goals. Just like your dad!"

"Like her dad?" Goh wondered out loud.

Chuck nodded, and he went on to tell a story about the first time he had met Bea. He had been visiting the Galar region in order to study Galar karate. While he was there, he had noticed the daughter of one of the assistant instructors. Even though the young girl barely reached the knees of the adults, she had powerful moves: high kicks, strong punches, and a very strong work ethic. That meant she knew it would take a lot of time, energy, and focus to become one of the best.

Ash and Goh could just picture a young Bea, tackling all the karate drills.

"She was widely known as a real up-and-coming talent in the art of Galar karate!" Chuck added. It was clear from the way he told the story that Bea had lived up to all the expectations others had for her. But maybe her own expectations were the greatest of all.

"To me, aiming to be the strongest—" Bea said between bites, "—was only natural!" She wiped some sweet cream from her lips. "So now, in order to be considered truly the strongest, I will defeat Leon."

"Well, I'm going to be the one to battle Leon first!" Ash insisted.

"We'll both work toward the goal of battling Leon," Bea stated.

"Right! We'll reach new heights!" Ash agreed.

"The two of you are aiming for the very same goal! My eyes are on you both!" Chuck said. "It will be immensely entertaining to see which of you winds up facing the undefeated Leon!"

"We will meet again . . . Riolu Trainer," Bea said.

"Hey—my name's Ash!" They all laughed, believing that the next time they met, Bea would not only remember Ash's Pokémon, but Ash as well.

Back at Professor Cerise's laboratory, Ash and Goh told the others all about their trip to the Johto region. "So it ended in a draw?" Professor Cerise asked. "Wow, that's too bad."

Ash was not as disappointed by the result as he would've thought. He still learned a lot during his showdown with Bea. "Next time, I'll win it!" Ash told everyone.

"Yes, I'll be cheering for you," Professor Cerise assured his young, ambitious research fellow. Then he turned to his other young research fellow. "Goh, by the way, what sort of Pokémon did you catch in Johto?"

"I'm really glad you asked!" Goh said. He had stayed true to his promise to himself—he had refused to get back on the yacht until he had captured a Pokémon that was unique to the Johto region. He had made all his traveling companions wait on the dock while he tried again and again.

"Come on out!" Goh called as he threw a Poké Ball.

"Oh! A Chinchou!" Professor Cerise said. He was impressed. The Pokémon lived underwater and had a round, blue body, plus-sign pupils in its yellow eyes, and special light-up antennae. It really was a rare addition to any collection!

"Not an easy catch, was it?" Ash said.

"Pika!"

"Rio!"

The whole crew had been relieved when Goh had finally reeled in a fresh Pokémon. Otherwise, they would probably all still be in Johto!

"But all's well! I actually *did* catch one!" Goh said, looking proud.

Even though there had not been a change in the World Coronation Series rankings, the trip to Johto had been a success! The second battle with Bea had given Ash a boost. He'd learned that not only do different Pokémon have different moves and battling styles, different Trainers did, too. It felt good to have a better sense of Bea and where she came from. It felt even better to know someone who shared his same goals.

For Ash, he knew he would always be striving to be the best Pokémon Trainer he could be. The World Coronation Series was just a new way to reach for that goal. Lucky for him, he was finding amazing, even mysterious, new Pokémon to share in the adventures—plus, he could always count on Pikachu to be his loyal partner. Every morning marked a fresh beginning. For this Pokémon Trainer, the journey starts today . . . every day!